For Donovan, whose voice will change the world. My love for you is endless. – A.L.

For James, June, and friends, who understand when words fail. – J.Z.

www.mascotbooks.com

Flap Your Wings, Little Robin

For more information, please contact:
Mascot Books
620 Herndon Parkway, Suite 320
Herndon, VA 20170
info@mascotbooks.com

Library of Congress Control Number: 2017913599

CPSIA Code: PBANG1117A
ISBN-13: 978-1-68401-597-9

Printed in the United States

Flap Your Wings, Little Robin

Written by Andrea Legg

Illustrated by Jenny Zandona

This is a story about a little robin.

A robin who looked like any other bird.

Acted like any other bird.

Sounded like — WAIT, no.

This little robin certainly didn't sound like any other bird.

In fact, he didn't sound like anything at all.

He couldn't tweet,
chirp, whistle, or hoot.

He couldn't hum, peep,
cluck, or even quack.

One morning, while farming for worms, the little robin stopped to rest on a fence post near a quiet barnyard.

"Howdy," said an old goat nearby, chewing some hay. "What brings you around these parts?"

The little robin froze. He wasn't used to other animals noticing him. He tried to whisper a hello, but as usual, nothing came out.

"Are you all right?" asked the old goat. The little robin nodded.

"It ain't like a bird to pass up a chance to make noise," the goat chuckled. "Haven't you got a voice?"

The little robin slowly shook his head.

The old goat thought for a minute. "I have an idea," he said. "Hop on my back."

The goat slowly trekked to a nearby wood with the little robin on his back, sniffing around like he'd been there before.

"Are you doing all right back there?" the goat asked the little robin.

The little robin patted the goat's back twice with his foot.

"I'm gonna take that as a yes," the old goat said.

Just then, the little robin heard a rustle in the bushes.

"Ol' Bear, is that you?" the old goat called out. "It's me, Goat."

The little robin watched, eyes wide, as an enormous brown bear crawled out from behind a tree. The little robin quivered and fanned out his wings in front of his chest.

"Goat! Good to see you," the bear beamed down at them. "What are you doing out here?"

"My friend Robin is having some trouble with his voice," the goat said. "Could you help him by showing him how you roar?"

The bear laughed. "Of course," he said, nodding to the little robin. "You just throw back your head like this and..."

The bear's roar shook the entire forest so completely that even the leaves on the trees trembled and the pebbles on the ground danced. The little robin fanned out his wings again, beak chattering.

"You try it," said the bear.

The little robin took a deep breath, threw his head back, and tried with all his might to roar just like the bear.

But nothing came out.

The little robin covered his eyes with his wings.

The bear looked puzzled and began pacing around the forest. "Aha!" the bear whooped. "I've got it."

The old bear whistled so loudly that the little robin jumped straight in the air.

Within seconds, a snake, an owl, and a cricket emerged from behind the bushes, peering out at their new visitors with wonder.

The bear smiled at the little robin. "These are the loudest animals in my forest. Maybe they can help you find your voice."

The bear turned to his friends. "Ready?" he asked.

"Sssssssssssssssssssssssssssssssssssssssss!" hissed the snake.

"Whoooooooooooooooooooooooooo!" sang the owl.

"Chirrrrrrrrrrp chirpchirpchirp, chirrrrrrrrrrrp," rang the cricket.

"Well?" The old goat flicked his tail. "Your turn."

The little robin puffed out his chest with hope and took a deep breath.
He threw his head back like the bear, stuck his tongue out like the
snake, blinked his eyes fast like the owl, and rubbed his wings together
like the cricket…

...but nothing came out.

The little robin covered his eyes with his wings again. Everyone was quiet.

Suddenly, the bear's head popped up. "Wait!" he cried. "Robin, when you stretch your wings out, does it mean you're...scared? I saw you do that after I roared."

The little robin lifted his head and nodded.

The old goat stopped chewing and turned to face the little robin. "And I saw you cover your eyes with your wings when you couldn't sing. Does that mean you're sad?"

The little robin looked over at the goat and nodded, his wings quickly flapping.

The bear waved his tree branch at the little robin's flapping wings and shouted, "Look, Goat! He flapped his wings! Did you see it?"

"Sure did!" said the goat.

The bear started pacing the forest again. "You're not scared," he muttered. "And you're not sad…"

He stopped. "Robin, are you...happy?"

The little robin looked around at his new friends who were trying so hard to understand him.

He felt a familiar warmth in his chest and nodded.

The little robin was happy.

"Don't you see, Robin? You've had a voice this whole time," said the old goat.

It was true.

He'd never be as loud as the other animals, and he'd never sing like the other robins. But he had friends who understood him.

And that's what mattered the most.

Learn to Sign Like Robin

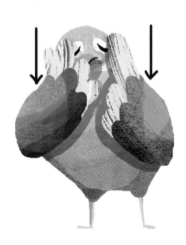

Happy

Sad

Scared

About the Author

Andrea Legg is a public librarian from northeastern Ohio whose writing has been featured on *Scary Mommy and The Mighty*. She is a member of the Ohio Library Council and the Society of Children's Book Writers and Illustrators. *Flap Your Wings, Little Robin* is her first book. To learn more, visit:

www.andrealegg.com

About the Illustrator

Jenny Zandona is an artist and illustrator hailing from the Pacific Northwest. Cultivation of her love of art and storytelling started from an early age when she would create superheroes and tales of kittens learning martial arts. Since then, Jenny's illustrations have continued to evolve, though her love of the strange and whimsical has never ceased. Jenny's work has been in exhibitions and published in multiple mediums, and she is thrilled to further indulge her passion for children's literature and illustration with *Flap Your Wings, Little Robin*. To learn more, visit:

www.jennyzandona.com